Robert C. Winthrop

An Address delivered at the Music Hall on the Evening of Fast Day, 7 April, 1859

Anatiposi

Robert C. Winthrop

An Address delivered at the Music Hall on the Evening of Fast Day, 7 April, 1859

Reprint of the original.

1st Edition 2023 | ISBN: 978-3-38230-556-7

Anatiposi Verlag is an imprint of Outlook Verlagsgesellschaft mbH.

Verlag (Publisher): Outlook Verlag GmbH, Zeilweg 44, 60439 Frankfurt, Deutschland
Vertretungsberechtigt (Authorized to represent): E. Roepke, Zeilweg 44, 60439 Frankfurt, Deutschland
Druck (Print): Books on Demand GmbH, In de Tarpen 42, 22848 Norderstedt, Deutschland

AN

ADDRESS

DELIVERED AT THE MUSIC HALL

ON THE EVENING OF

FAST DAY, 7 APRIL, 1859.

BEFORE THE

YOUNG MEN'S CHRISTIAN ASSOCIATION

OF BOSTON.

BY

ROBERT C. WINTHROP.

BOSTON:

LITTLE, BROWN AND COMPANY.

M DCCC LIX.

INTRODUCTION.

THE following Discourse, delivered in Boston on the 7th of April, was repeated on the evening of May 5th, 1859, at the African Church in Richmond, Virginia, before the Young Men's Christian Association of that city. A few local references were, of course, modified in conformity with the change of place; but no alteration was made of any substantial principle, precept, or even phrase, to meet the variations of latitude or longitude. It was originally prepared with a view to delivery in both cities, and in compliance with frequent solicitations from both Associations.

It is now published in conformity with a united and only too flattering appeal from both Associations; and is respectfully dedicated to the young men composing them, with the earnest hope that they may cherish the interests of a common Christianity, which shall have but one voice for the North and for the South, and which shall promote the permanent welfare of all to whom it is addressed.

The occasion at Richmond was introduced by some eloquent remarks from William P. Munford, Esq., (the President of the Richmond Association,) of which no copy is at hand.

At Boston, the President of the Association, Mr. Franklin W. Smith, introduced the exercises of the evening, as follows :—

"The Boston Young Men's Christian Association, most gratefully appreciate the kindness of the honorable gentleman, who has consented to speak this evening, in behalf of the Building Fund. Several months since he manifested substantially his interest in the object; and now we have further proof of his kind and earnest desire for its promotion.

"It cannot be doubted, that this large audience, which has assembled so eagerly to listen to his discourse, will likewise sympathize with its purpose : and it may be therefore desirable, briefly and practically, to explain the design of the present effort to raise a permanent fund.

"The only reliable income of the Association, has been from its annual memberships; which at present number about one thousand at one dollar each. The assessment is made thus moderate in amount, that admission may be available to young men of the humblest pecuniary means. During the seven years of its existence, the required outlay for rent, salary of librarian, for books, periodicals, and contingent expenses, has been about three thousand dollars per annum. The deficit has always been supplied by the ready liberality of its friends. But to avoid the necessity of an annual subscription to meet a constantly recurring debt, it was deemed expedient, at the commencement of the present year, to obtain a fund of twenty-five thousand dollars. Said fund to be held in trust by four gentlemen of the various denominations represented in the Association; the interest thereon to be applied to the rent of its rooms, or the principal to be invested in a building adapted to its use, at their discretion.

"Through the successful result of the late Fair, held in behalf of this object, and by a subscription prosecuted within a few months past, which has received a most liberal response, about sixteen thousand dollars of the amount desired, has been obtained.

"I have great pleasure in introducing to the audience, the Hon. ROBERT C. WINTHROP."

ADDRESS.

I AM not altogether without apprehension, Mr. President, in rising to perform the service for which you have so kindly announced me, that an Address originally intended only as a plain and frank declaration of old-fashioned opinions, and more particularly as an earnest of my sincere sympathy with the Young Men who have honored me with an invitation to speak to them this evening, may fail of meeting the expectations of many of those whom I see around me. But I am here for no personal display, for no secular, rhetorical discourse. I yield the palm of eloquence without a struggle or a sigh, to those who already, during the present week, have waked the echoes of this hall, and of other halls in its vicinity, to a marvellous and magical music of words and thoughts to which I can make so little pretension. Coming here on the evening of a day which has been set apart in conformity with ancient usage for exercises of religion, and coming at the instance and for the furtherance of an association instituted for religious improvement, I shall not decline or evade the direct subject presented to me

by the occasion, the audience, and the object. And if
I shall have succeeded in awakening a worthier motive,
or kindling a nobler aspiration, or prompting a more
generous impulse in any youthful heart, I shall be better
rewarded than if I could have won the richest garland
of the Olympian Games.

I know not, my friends, precisely by whom, or under
what circumstances, the original idea of associations, like
that which I have the honor to address this evening,
was first suggested, or under what auspices that idea
found its earliest practical fulfilment. It is said to have
been in the city of London, in the year 1844, where some
of the most eminent statesmen of the British realm have
alternated with the clergy of all denominations, in deliv-
ering successive courses of lectures on moral and religious topics before a similar association. But I can con-
ceive of few more enviable distinctions which any man,
young or old, could claim for himself, than to have been
the original founder or the original proposer of such an
organization. Nor, in my humble judgment, could any
city of our own land, or of any other land, present a
higher title to the grateful consideration of all good men,
than that city, wherever it may be, within whose limits
and under whose auspices, the first Young Men's Christian Association, or Union, was successfully organized
and established.

The ancient metropolis of Syria has secured for itself
a manifold celebrity on the pages of history. It has
been celebrated as the splendid residence of the Syrian
kings, and afterwards as the luxurious capital of the
Asiatic Provinces of the Roman Empire. It has been

celebrated for its men of letters, and its cultivation of
learning. It has been celebrated for the magnificence
of the edifices within its walls, and for the romantic
beauty of its suburban groves and fountains. The cir-
cling sun shone nowhere upon more majestic productions
of human art, than when it gilded, with its rising or
its setting beams, the sumptuous symbols of its own de-
luded worshippers, in the gorgeous temple of Daphne
and the gigantic statue of Apollo, which were the pride
and boast of that far-famed capital ; while it was from
one of the humble hermitages which were embosomed
in its exquisite environs, that the sainted Chrysostom
poured forth some of those poetical and passionate rap-
tures on the beauties and sublimities of nature, which
would alone have won for him the title of "the golden-
mouthed." At one time, we are told, it ranked *third* on
the list of the great cities of the world,—next only after
Rome and Alexandria, and hardly inferior to the latter
of the two, at least, in size and splendor. It acquired a
severer and sadder renown in more recent, though still
remote history, as having been doomed to undergo vicis-
situdes and catastrophes of the most disastrous and deplorable character ;—now sacked and pillaged by the
Persians, now captured by the Saracens, and now be-
sieged by the Crusaders ; a prey, at one moment, to
the ravages of fire,—at another, to the devastations of
an earthquake, which is said to have destroyed no less
than two hundred and fifty thousand human lives in a
single hour. Its name has thus become associated with
so many historical lights and shadows,—with so much of
alternate grandeur and gloom,—that there is, perhaps,

but little likelihood of its ever being wholly lost sight of
by any student of antiquity. Yet it is not too much to
say, that one little fact, for which the Bible is the sole
and all-sufficient authority, will fix that name in the
memory, and rivet it in the affectionate regard of mankind, when all else associated with it is forgotten. Yes,
when its palaces and its temples, its fountains and its
groves, its works of art and its men of learning, when
Persian and Saracen and Crusader, who successively
spoiled it, and the flames and the earthquake which de-
voured and desolated it, shall have utterly faded from all
human recollection or record, the little fact—the great
fact, let me rather say—will still be remembered, and
remembered with an interest and a vividness which no
time can ever efface or diminish,—that "the Disciples
were called Christians first in Antioch;" that there the
name of Christ,—given at the outset, perhaps, as a nick-
name and a by-word, but gladly and fearlessly accepted
and adopted, in the face of mockery, in the face of mar-
tyrdom, by delicate youth and maiden tenderness, as
well as by mature or veteran manhood,—first became
the distinctive designation of the faithful followers of
the Messiah.

That record must, of course, stand alone, forever, on
the historic page. Christianity will never begin again.
Christ has lived and died once for all, and will come no
more upon these earthly scenes, until he comes again in
his glorious majesty to judge both the quick and the dead.
But, should the numerous Associations and Unions
which have recently sprung into existence as from a
common impulse in both hemispheres,—bearing a com-

mon name, composed of congenial elements, and organized for the same great and glorious ends with that now before me,—should they go on zealously and successfully in the noble work which they have undertaken,—should they even fulfil but one half the high hopes and fond expectations which their progress thus far has authorized and encouraged,—it may be, it may be, that the city from which they all took their first example and origin, if it can then be identified,—whether it be London or New York,—Liverpool, Edinburgh, or Boston,—Berlin, Geneva, or Richmond,—will have no prouder or loftier title to the gratitude of man or to the blessing of God, than that there was set on foot the first Young Men's Christian Association,—that there the young men of the nineteenth century, by a concerted movement, and in so considerable companies, first professed and called themselves Christians.

Certainly, certainly, my friends, it is no common event in the history of the moral and religious progress of mankind, that the young men of so many of the great cities of the world should have simultaneously arrayed and organized themselves under the distinctive banner of the Cross, and should have openly adopted the baptismal designation of Christian Associations. The great body of young men, in almost all ages and countries, have, I need hardly say, been proverbially accustomed to shrink from anything like Christian professions. They have thought it well enough for the old, perhaps,—after the pleasures and vanities of life had been exhausted,—to turn their attention to the grave and sober concerns of religion. They have recognized the good policy, doubt-

less, of beginning to devise means for securing safety
and happiness in another world, when little or nothing
more remained to be enjoyed or expected in this. But
to be called pious, or even serious, in youth, has often
been resented as a term of downright disparagement
and reproach ;—while to have enlisted in the open ranks
of a Christian Association would have been regarded,
even by some of those present, not many years ago,
as indicating a total and most deplorable lack of that
manly, generous, and chivalrous spirit which could alone
be relied on to render young men honorable, enterpris-
ing, useful, or even respectable in life.

And it must be admitted, in all candor, that young
men, just emerging from the restraints of parental or
scholastic discipline,—with so much hot blood leaping
in their veins, and with so many cherished visions of
independent life dancing and glittering before their view,
—are not in the best condition to form a wise and safe
decision on matters of this sort. Nor can it be greatly
wondered at, that even if they are led, like their mem-
orable prototype in the Scripture, to come to the Master
and inquire what they shall do to inherit eternal life,—
so many of them should be found, like him, going away,
—exceeding sorrowful at first, it may be,—but still going
away,—perhaps never again to return.

More especially is this liable to be the case with
young men, whose lot in life is cast by Providence, or
cast by parental preference, or cast of their own choice,
amid the crowded marts and busy throngs and confused
thoroughfares of some proud and luxurious metropolis.
Who marvels that the hearts of the most hopeful Chris-

tians have so often grown faint and almost sunk in
despair within them, as they have contemplated the dis-
tractions and temptations which belong to a large city!
In the quiet seclusion of a country life, a virtuous and
religious course seems comparatively easy. The pure
atmosphere of the open fields supplies health to the soul
as well as to the body. Rural occupation invigorates the
moral as well as the muscular system. The unobstructed
contemplation of the earth and the heavens, and the habitual observation of the marvellous course of the sun and
the seasons, inspire a thoughtful reverence for the great
Creator. A drought or a freshet, defying the best energies of man to avert their desolating influences,—blasting
in a month, or it may be in a moment, the whole promise
of the year,—inculcates a lesson of constant dependence
upon God, which no heedlessness and no presumption
can altogether deride or disregard. In the country, too,
the week-day labors are more rarely interrupted by the
noise of feasting and revelry; and the opportunities for
evening indulgence and dissipation, if not entirely un-
known, are of comparatively infrequent occurrence. And
there, also, the solemn stillness of the day of rest, broken
only by the sweet music of the village bell or the tuneful
melodies of the village choir, invites both young and old,
with no doubtful or divided appeal, to the worship of
God in his holy temple.

But how many of these blessed influences are enfeebled and paralyzed, if not wholly wanting, in "proud,
and gay and gain-devoted cities!" There, art seems to
aim at, and almost to accomplish, the work of shutting
out from sight the whole face of nature. There, the

steam and smoke and dust of varied and incessant labor
seem to blur over and blot out more than half the
heavens from the spiritual as well as from the natural
eye. There, everything speaks of man, and nothing of
God. There, wealth too often engenders a corrupting
and cankering luxury, and opportunities and examples of
vicious indulgence are multiplied at every corner. Well
does the thoughtful Cowper exclaim, in one of those
charming poems, in the perusal of which our own
Franklin tells us that he revived his long-lost " relish
for reading poetry":—

> " In cities, vice is hidden with most ease,
> Or seen with least reproach."

Well does he add :—

> " Rank abundance breeds,
> In pampered cities, sloth and lust,
> And wantonness and gluttonous excess."

And there, too, the dizzying whirl of business and
amusement, by which men are hurried along through the
six days which are avowedly given to the world, leaves
them too frequently with but jaded and distracted souls
for the one day which is nominally dedicated to the Lord;
and the services of the sanctuary are too often attended
with listless indifference, or forsaken altogether, upon
pretences of health or of weather, which would not have
detained them a moment from a ball, a concert, or an
opera.

" Let us endeavor,—said that great statesman and
orator, Edmund Burke, writing from Dublin, at sixteen
years of age, to his schoolfellow, Richard Shackleton,—

'Let us endeavor to live according to the rules of the Gospel; and He that prescribed them, I hope, will consider our endeavors to please Him, and assist us in our designs.' This, my friend, is your advice, and how hard is it for me to follow it! I am in the enemy's country, —the townsman is beset on every side. It is here difficult to sit down to think seriously. Oh! how happy are you who live in the country! I assure you, my friend, that without the superior grace of God, I will find it very difficult to be commonly virtuous."

What heart in this assembly—young or old—does not respond to reflections like these? Who can contemplate the manifestations of human frailty and human depravity, as daily and hourly presented to our view even on the mere surface-life of a great city, without feeling deeply and painfully the dangers to which the young and inexperienced are exposed within its walls? And yet, my friends, how small a part of those dangers is visible to the human eye! How very small a proportion of all the vices and crimes which are committed within the walls of a crowded metropolis, is ever brought to the knowledge of any human tribunal! How few of the sins over which angels may be weeping, ever reach the criminal calendar or the public journal! How much of "rioting and drunkenness," how much of "chambering and wantonness," how many frauds and forgeries, suicides and infanticides, how many excesses and violences and villanies of every sort, go along, not merely unwhipped of justice, but absolutely undivulged! How many crimes remain to be exposed and audited in another world, for the one which now and then startles and shocks us in this world, by the monstrous details of its grossness and its guilt!

Reflect, my friends, for an instant, what a spectacle almost any great city would present, at almost any single moment of its existence, to a person who had the power to penetrate within its recesses and privacies, and to behold at a glance all that was going on by day or by night within its limits! Nay, reflect, if you have the courage to do so, what a spectacle such a city actually does present to that all-seeing Eye, before which every scene of immorality and crime is daguerreotyped with unfailing accuracy and minuteness—just as it occurs—just as it occurs—no matter how close may be the veil of mystery in which it is involved to human sight, or how secret the chambers of iniquity within which it is transacted! What a panorama must be ever moving before that Eye! Oh, if there could be a more prevailing and pervading sense, that although no human agency or visible machinery be at work, the picture of our individual lives is at every instant in process of being portrayed and copied—every word, act, thought, motive, indelibly delineated, with a fulness and a fidelity of which even the marvellous exactness of photograph or stereoscope affords but a faint illustration;—if the great ideas of Omniscience and Omnipresence, which are suffered to play so loosely about the region of our imaginations, and of which these modern inventions—the daguerreotype, with the instantaneous action and unerring accuracy of its viewless pencil, —the Electric Ocean Telegraph, with its single flash, bounding unquenched through a thousand leagues of fathomless floods,—have done so much to quicken our feeble conceptions;—if, I say, these great ideas of Omniscience and Omnipresence could now and then be brought to a focus, and flashed in, with the full force of their searching and scorching rays, upon the inmost soul of some great city, like Paris or London,—to come no nearer home,—and of those who dwell in it;—what swarms of sins, what troops of sinners, would be seen scared and scampering from their holes and hiding-places;—just as even now the inmates of some single abode of iniquity or infamy are sometimes seen flying from the sudden irruption of an earthly police, or from the startling terrors of some self-constituted vigilance committee!

What a different scene would some of the great cities of our own land, as well as of other lands, present,—what new securities should we enjoy for morality, for liberty, for property, for everything which is comprised in the idea of public or private virtue,—could there be cherished and cultivated by us all, such an habitual and vivid sense of an ever-watchful Eye, piercing through all disguises and from which no secrets are hid,—as that which the immortal Milton bears witness to in his own breast, in closing the account of those youthful travels on the Continent,—where he had not only conversed with Galileo and Grotius, and been complimented and flattered and caressed by cardinals and courtiers, and by all the leading luminaries of those countless fantastic Academies of Literature and Science with which Italy then swarmed, —with the Bees of Rome at their head,—the Humorists and the Melancholics, the Disordered and the Disgusted, the Idlers, the Indifferents, the Neglected and the Bewildered,—but where he had been fascinated too by the surpassing song of Leonora Baroni, and had tasked his Tuscan to the utmost in composing sonnets in admiration of some nameless beauty of Bologna, and had lingered and luxuriated in that voluptuous atmosphere of Nature and of Art, which often puts the sternest virtue to the test :—" I again take God to witness, (said he, in closing that tour, and the passage also forms the close of the just published volume of his new and noble biography,) I again take God to witness, that in all those places where so many things are considered lawful, I lived sound and untouched from all profligacy and vice, having this thought perpetually with me, that though I might escape the eyes of man, I certainly could not escape the eyes of God!"

It cannot be denied that more than one of our own American cities, limited as they still are in population, in wealth, and in luxury, when compared with the ancient capitals of the old world,—and imbued as more than one of them still is, we trust, with that regard for morality and that reverence for religion which were the peculiar characteristics of their founders,—have exhibited of late some fearful indications of enfeebled principle and declining virtue. It cannot be denied, that now and then,— when the detection and investigation of some appalling crime have withdrawn the curtain, for a moment, from the domestic life of some of our wealthy capitals,—scenes have been disclosed which make us shudder at the bare imagination of what that curtain may still conceal. And how often must the solemn reflection have occurred to many a father's and many a mother's heart, when called

upon to trust their sons and their daughters to go forth,
in pursuit of education or occupation, beyond the limits
of parental supervision,—"Amid what scenes and surroundings are my children about to be cast! Into what
depths of worldliness and sensuality and sin may they
not be plunged! How, how, are they to be screened
and shielded from these tremendous perils? How can
the force of association and example, and the influence of
fraternity and friendship,—the contagion of good fellow-
ship,—the electric cord of social sympathy,—be employed
to lead them in the way of safety and of virtue, as they
are now so often employed in seducing them into paths
of folly and of crime?" And how must the hearts of such
parents have been relieved, encouraged, and gladdened by
the sudden and simultaneous appearance, in so many of
our largest cities, of such Associations as that which I
now address,—instituted from nothing less, I am per-
suaded, than a Divine impulse, and organized by the
young men themselves, to animate and aid each other
in the perilous paths which they are called on to tread
together! What parent, what Christian, what patriot,—
what lover of virtue or lover of his country,—can withhold
from such Associations whatever of moral or of material
aid it may be in his power to offer them? Who, especially, could refuse to lend them, at their call, the
humble tribute of a few words of sympathy, encourage-
ment, and friendly counsel? For myself, Mr. President
and Brethren, (for I cannot forget that from the earliest
day of your existence I have been enrolled among your
life members,) for myself,—declining, as I have done
of late, a great majority of the invitations with which I

have been honored to deliver Lectures, Addresses, and
Orations,—deeply conscious, moreover, of my own insuf-
ficiency for giving the desired and deserved attractiveness
to this particular occasion, and sincerely sensible that there
are many others around me at this moment who could do
a hundred times better justice to its only appropriate
topics,—I should yet have felt that my voice was unworthy to be heard henceforth forever in any public
service or for any popular use, if I had refused it longer
to your repeated solicitations.

And now, my friends, I have already sufficiently in-
dicated, in these introductory remarks, the most important
view which I take of this Association, namely, as a vol-
untary organization of the very persons most exposed to
danger, and in the very places where dangers are most
frequent and most fatal, for their own mutual protection ;
a volunteer corps, if I may so speak, for moral and spiritual self-defence ; and one of the questions which is to
be asked before I close, is whether this volunteer corps
—this new battalion—shall not be furnished with a com-
modious and convenient armory ?—I can add nothing
to the simple statement of this great leading idea. It is
too obvious to every one to require, or even admit of,
further illustration. Let me then avail myself of what
remains of the time which I may reasonably, or even
unreasonably, occupy this evening, by speaking simply
and plainly of that great and crying want in our individual and in our social condition, which the influence
of these Associations is so eminently adapted to supply ;
—I mean the want of more, of a great deal more, of true

Christian spirit, and Christian motive, and Christian principle, in all the various affairs and transactions and enterprises of the world we live in, and for the sake of the world we live in.—For there are two distinct views of the influence of Christian professions and a Christian life ;—the one, as they prepare the individual man for the great responsibilities and retributions of the world to come ;—the other, as they fit him for a wiser and better and worthier discharge of the world that now is. I leave the first of these views wholly to the pulpit, and I trust I shall not be thought to trench too much on the rightful prerogative of the pulpit in a brief allusion to the other. I trust too, most earnestly, that I shall not be thought to imply any particle of disrespect for those who occupy the sacred office,—the highest which any mortal man can hold,—an ambassadorship more exalted than any which can be derived from earthly thrones or potentates, however imposing the ceremonial of their courts, or however imperial the extent of their dominions,—if I intimate, in the first place, that there is room for more of a Christian spirit even in maintaining and pleading and prosecuting the very cause of Christianity itself.

Religious intolerance and persecution, so far as the operation of laws and of government is concerned, have in so great a degree disappeared during the present century, in our own land, at least, that we are accustomed to consider our own condition as peculiarly one of religious as well as civil liberty. And so it is. But let us not forget, that there may be a *spirit* of religious bitterness and bigotry pervading a community, which is as unworthy of those who entertain it,—although it be

not so oppressive upon those towards whom it is directed,
—as that which is conducted through the forms of law.
And few persons, I think, can contemplate even the present improved condition of the Christian world in this
respect, without lamenting that the best energies of
Christian sects are still so often employed in criticizing,
censuring, and condemning each other. No considerate
and candid man, I think, can help regretting that any
portion of the time set apart for religious instruction and
exhortation should be directly or indirectly devoted to the
inculcation of jealousies and hostilities among those who
take different views of the teachings of the Sacred Scrip-
tures. It is time that the *odium theologicum* should
cease to be a proverb and a by-word, and that religious
hatred should no longer be a synonyme for the sternest
and most implacable of all human hatreds. I pray
Heaven, that no accident, and still more that no design,
may revive the slumbering embers of religious strife in
our own community. Rarely, rarely, does the strongest
side prevail, or even come off best, from such encounters.
Not often does even the right side, whether it be strongest or weakest, escape from them without damage or
detriment. Principles, indeed, can never be conceded
nor compromised. We can never abandon the Bible,
even in the schools. We can never compromise the
Lord's Prayer or the Ten Commandments. We cannot
spare a note or a chord of the time-honored and glorious
harmonies of Old Hundred. Yet everything except
principles, everything that is merely formal and conventional, may well be the subject of conciliatory arrange-
ment, under proper circumstances and at the proper time,
for the sake of Christian peace.

I have few more delightful reminiscences of foreign travel, nearly twelve years since, than a visit to the model school of Dublin, in company with, and under the immediate escort of, that great living Protestant thinker and writer, Archbishop Whately, where a thousand pupils, paying each one, I believe, a penny a day, were educated side by side, Protestant and Roman Catholic alike, some of them studying out of Jacob Abbott's school-books, and all of them reading lessons from the Bible, as arranged between Whately himself,—the very author of the " Errors of Romanism,"—and the Roman Catholic Archbishop of Dublin. If such a spectacle is not to continue to be witnessed either there or here, let it not be, I pray Heaven, the result of a revival of religious animosity on our part ;—let it not be, I pray Heaven, because Christian ministers or Christian men have fanned a flame and kindled a conflagration which it may be beyond their power to extinguish, when they themselves would be most glad to do so. Let us rather try, " By winning words to conquer willing "—or even unwilling—" hearts, and make persuasion do the work of fear."

If the noblest and worthiest definition of Deity be that " God is love,"—if the final test and touchstone of discipleship be that which Christ himself so impressively prescribed in his parting precept, " By this shall all men know that ye are my disciples, if ye have *love* one to another,"—how imperative is the obligation which rests upon us all to see to it, that not alone from the written or printed page of the Statute Book, but from the fleshly tables of our own hearts, every root and remnant of religious enmity and animosity should disappear forever !

Was it not nobly as well as exquisitely said by Jeremy
Taylor, in his celebrated discourse before the University
of Dublin, " Theology is rather a divine life, than a
divine knowledge. In heaven, indeed, we shall first see,
and then love; but here on earth, we must first love, and
love will open our eyes as well as our hearts; and we
shall then see, perceive, and understand."

For one, my friends, I can never think of the bitterness and rancor which is so often allowed to enter into
religious differences and religious controversies, without
remembering how much our religious opinions, our religious creeds, our religious connections, have been determined,—pre-determined, providentially determined,—for
us all, by the mere influence of early and seemingly
accidental associations. The place of our birth, the circumstances of our condition, the surroundings of our
childhood, the fascination of some beloved and faithful
pastor, the paternal precept and example, the mother's
knee, the family pew, have, after all, done more to decide
for each one of us the peculiarities of our religious faith
and of our religious forms, than all the catechisms of
assemblies, the decrees of councils, or the canons of con-
vocations. We delight to worship God where our fathers
and mothers worshipped him, to kneel at the same altar
at which they knelt, to unite in the same prayers, or, it
may be, to utter the same responses, in which their voices
were once heard, and which they first taught us to lisp
or to listen to as children. The memories of fathers and
mothers and brothers and sisters, with whom we have
" taken sweet counsel together, and walked to the house
of God in company," cluster sweetly around us as we sit

in the old seats and sing the old psalms and hymns. We
almost shrink from trying to get to heaven by any other
road than that which they travelled, lest we should miss
them at our journey's end. And is he not a very unwise
person, who, without some deep and overpowering con-
viction, would rudely break the spell and dissolve the
charm of such associations, either for himself or others?
How miserable is it then, to allow the differences which
have an origin so natural, so worthy, so hallowed, so
providential, to become the subject of mutual suspicions,
reproaches, and denunciations!

It is well for us all to remember, that, in the language
of my Lord Bacon, " they be two things—unity and uni-
formity." And how admirably does he suggest in his
essay on " Unity in Religion,"—" A man that is of
judgment and understanding shall sometimes hear igno-
rant men differ, and know well within himself, that those
which so differ mean one thing, and yet they themselves
would never agree; and if it come so to pass in that
distance of judgment which is between man and man,
shall we not think that God above, that knows the heart,
doth not discern that frail men in some of their contra-
dictions, intend the same thing, and accepteth both?"

Doubtless, every man who has opportunity and education should read the Gospel of Christ for himself, and
bring the best lights within his reach to aid him in its
interpretation. But mysteries there are in that Gospel,
which constrained even the great apostle to say, "Here
we see as through a glass, darkly." Mysteries there are,
like those which made the mightiest intellect of our land
and age,—which I have often seen bend itself reverently

at the communion table of a Washington or a Boston
Church,—prescribe for the legend of his own tombstone
at Marshfield, as the very preamble of a declaration of
faith in " the Gospel of Christ as a Divine Reality," and
in " the Sermon on the Mount as more than a merely
human production,"—those touching words of the father
of the tormented child which was brought unto Jesus to
be cured, " Lord, I believe—help thou mine unbelief."
Mysteries there are, which the reason of the natural man
was never made or intended to penetrate, which, it may
be, were expressly designed to humble the presumption
and confound the pride and mortify the vanity of mere
human wisdom, and to leave larger room for the childlike
graces of humility and faith; and the speculative differences, which such mysteries must ever and inevitably
engender, should be regarded with mutual deference and
charity,—never forgetting that it were an impeachment
of the love of God, and an imputation upon the mercy
of Christ, to imagine, that the essential elements of a
true Christian faith have been placed beyond the easy
reach and ready acceptance even of the humblest and
simplest understanding. It were, indeed, to turn into a
mere mockery that prophetic declaration, whose fulfilment
was one of the chosen and infallible evidences of his
divine mission and Messiahship, and which was recalled
as such, by the answer of Christ himself, to the remembrance of the inquiring Baptist as he lay pining in
prison—" The spirit of the Lord is upon me, because
he hath anointed me to preach the Gospel to the poor,"
—it were, I say, to turn *this preaching of the Gospel
to the poor* into a mere juggling mockery,—keeping it

to the ear, but breaking it to the hope,—to set up as shibboleths of the straight gate, upon any mere human authority or construction, metaphysical formulas and dogmas, which even men who have had leisure, and men who have had learning, philosophers and linguists and closet students, have disputed and wrangled about for centuries, without coming any nearer to a satisfactory solution of their own doubts and disagreements, and of which the poor, the unlearned, the toiling millions of mankind can never have any adequate comprehension or conception.

I hail this union of Young Men of so many different Christian sects, in a single Association, for Christian ends and objects, as a pledge that the jealousies and rivalries which have so long divided the Church of Christ on earth, will be more and more assuaged and extinguished, —that religious men of all denominations will more and more bear in mind the great and glorious things in which they all agree, and will strive to narrow instead of widening their causes of alienation and estrangement. The day may come, and I fear is even now not a great way off, when the cause of Christianity may require and demand the cordial and vigorous union of all who acknowledge God as their Father, and Christ as their Redeemer and Saviour, and the Bible as the word of God and the only text-book of eternal truth, in order to withstand and resist the progress of a downright infidelity,—cloaking itself under a thousand specious forms of positive and speculative philosophy, of materialism, spiritualism, and pantheism. Let us prepare seasonably for such a day, and for the conflicts it will involve, by uniting together in

a league of Christian charity,—holding our faith in the
unity of the Spirit, and in the bond of peace. Let us pur-
sue our Christian work in the true spirit of Christianity,
—a spirit of love to God and of love to man,—maintaining our peculiar and distinctive tenets firmly but never
arrogantly, boldly but never offensively, uncompromis-
ingly, if you please, but never aggressively,—ever respect-
ing our neighbor's conscience as we claim our neighbor's
respect for our own conscience, and not forgetting that
our final responsibilities are not to each other, but to that
common Master before whom we must stand or fall.
Who does not rejoice, as Sunday after Sunday comes
round, to see the multitudes that keep holy day thronging
our streets and sidewalks, and exchanging the smiles of
recognition or the greetings of friendship or the formal-
ities of ceremony, as they make way for each other in
passing along to their various places of religious worship?
To human eyes, indeed, they seem to be moving in widely
different directions, and so it may prove to have been with
some of them. But so have I seen on a summer sea, in
yonder bay, alike in calm and in storm, vessels of every
sort and beneath every sign, sailing in widely different
and diverging courses, crossing and recrossing each
others' tracks, and seemingly propelled by the most opposite and contrarious forces. Yet the same wind of
heaven, blowing where it listeth, was the common source
of their motive power, giving impulse and direction to
the progress of them all alike, and bringing them all to
be moored at last in one common haven of rest!

But if passing from the religious, we glance, for an
instant, at the moral movements of the age, I think we

may perceive a still more imperative demand for something more of Christian spirit and motive and principle, on the part of not a few of those by whom they are conducted. Indeed, I know of few things more deplorable in our day and generation than the tone and temper,—I should rather say, the want of temper,—which characterize so much of our moral controversy. It would seem to be thought in some quarters, that any degree of violence and vituperation will be justified and sanctified, if they are only employed in a good cause. Intemperate declaimers in favor of Temperance, pugnacious advocates for Peace, and pleaders for human Liberty, whose great art and part would seem to be to take liberties of the most unwarrantable kind with the characters and motives of all who dare to differ from them, have been found at every corner of our streets. Mere worldly instrumentalities, too, are relied upon almost exclusively for advancing the great reforms of society. Associations and agitations, political combinations and human legislation,—to say nothing even of the bludgeon or the bowie-knife, the revolver or the rifle,—are invoked and appealed to as the all-sufficient agencies for remedying the evils or redressing the wrongs of our social condition ;—while Christian prayer and Christian faith are disparaged, and in some quarters, at least, discarded and derided as worthless and impotent. But for one, I have no confidence in the pursuit of Christian ends by unchristian means. I have no belief that the way to advance virtue is to ignore its only foundation, or the way to promote justice or truth to set society by the ears and the whole world in a flame. For myself, I can only say, that I would sooner rely for the success of any great reform upon what one of the apostles calls, " the effectual fervent prayer " of one righteous man, than on the agitations and clamors of a hundred thousand fanatics, disclaiming all regard for Christianity and denouncing its churches and its ministry. God has never promised success to agencies like these. It is faith which is to remove mountains; and prayer, which is the only true earnest and exercise of faith, is the very lever by which mountains are to be removed. By faith, I need not say, my friends, that I mean no vain, presumptuous belief in one's self and in one's own power and might,—no heathenish self-confidence, like that expressed in the old classical motto: " They can, because they believe they can ;"—but I mean a belief in the power and promises of God, and in the revelations of his word and will. This was the sort of faith which Paul spoke of, when he described the great heroes and prophets of the Old Testament, as having " through *faith* subdued kingdoms, wrought righteousness, obtained promises, stopped the mouth of lions, quenched the violence of fire, escaped the edge of the sword." It was faith in God which accomplished these wonders in the olden time, and it is faith in God and in Christ which is primarily to accomplish whatever moral reforms are to be achieved in our own day. But the only faith which too many modern reformers seem to consider important, is *faith in themselves,*—faith in their own infallibility, their own virtue, justice, and consummate ability and wisdom ;—and by this alone they think to carry everything before them. Impatient of the slow processes by which the greatest designs of Providence are often unfolded, matured, and

accomplished,—spurning that old expectant system which
David illustrated so exquisitely in one of his most familiar
psalms, " I waited patiently for the Lord, and he inclined
unto me and heard my calling,"—they are ever adopting
a sort of heroic practice for bringing their projects to an
issue. They would almost seem to be jealous lest the
Almighty himself should get the start of them in effecting
his purposes of mercy, justice, and love, among the children of men. They aim at all reformation in the condition of their fellow-beings, as if mere earthly and temporal inferiority and infirmity and suffering were the only
evils worthy of consideration, as if there were no world
but this world for the grievances of humanity to be re-
dressed in, and nobody to redress those grievances but
weak and impotent man. In a word, they shut their
own eyes, and would seem disposed to shut other people's
eyes, to the great fact, that the only true reformers are
those who aim, as you are aiming, to advance God's
glory and Christ's kingdom on earth ;—and that when
that kingdom shall fully come, in answer to the prayers
and efforts of a Christian world, War, Slavery, Intem-
perance, and every other real or seeming evil, will vanish
before it like darkness before the dawn, and that just as
its coming is hastened and its nearness increased, will be
the proportionate success of all human efforts in favor of
relieving the woes and promoting the general welfare of
mankind. " Seek ye first the kingdom of God, and his
righteousness, and all these things shall be added unto
you." This is the Heaven-descended rule and law of
moral progress as well as of personal prosperity and success, and there is no other law.

I do not forget that enthusiasm and zeal have been elements in the character of real reformers as well as of charlatans and pretenders,—of St. Paul and of Luther, as well as of Mahomet or Joe Smith. I would not undervalue the earnestness and fearlessness which characterize the efforts of so many a false apostle, as well as of so many a true one. I would not even question the sincerity of anybody. But what I do say, is, that the enthusiasm and zeal which are not under the constant regulation and control of Christian principle, and which are not in constant subordination to the revealed word and will of God, are only like so much steam in an engine without a valve or a governor, propelling a vessel without a pilot or an engineer. If that vessel be not sooner or later dashed to pieces upon the rocks, it will only be because it has been exploded into thin air, before it reaches them, or because it has been left already a smouldering hulk upon the waters!

Turn with me now, once more, for a moment, to the business affairs of daily life, and tell me if here, also, there be not manifest need of a more Christian spirit, and of a higher and deeper sense of Christian duty and obligation. Do not the hourly transactions of a great commercial emporium, (not to speak particularly or invidiously of our own,) afford ample proof, as they pass under review in the columns of a morning or an evening paper, that more, a great deal more, of religious principle might fitly find a place in every department of human occupation? Look at the fluctuation of stocks and at the operations of some of those who thrive upon their rise and fall; consider the contrivances of the money-changers, as they lie in wait to take advantage of the exigencies of the needy ; follow the footsteps of a hundred speculators as they rush along in a wild pursuit of wealth for themselves, while they care not for involving their neighbors in ruin ; reflect on the wretchedness and crime so often engendered by practices, compared with which the hugging of real *bears* and the goring of real *bulls* would be merciful towards their miserable dupes ; mark the multiplying instances of embezzlement and defalcation, or recall the stupendous frauds, which have startled whole communities from the slumber of false confidence in which they had hitherto so fatally reposed,—and into which, alas ! a new penal statute, or an increased detective police, or a more frequent investigation of books and balances, emboldens them so soon to relapse !

Passing from the Exchange, enter next the very halls of justice, and observe some of the processes for punishing crime, or for establishing right between man and man. Do not confine your attention, either, to the prisoner at the bar, or to the parties to the suit. Attend to the witnesses ; hearken to the jury; listen to the advocates themselves, and take note of the mode of cross-examination, and to the arguments and appeals of counsel. Is there all the old confidence that there is no trifling with oaths, no tampering with testimony, no systematic concealment or distortion of truth, no wholesale fabrication of falsehood, in the management of modern trials? Is there not even room for the apprehension that the contests of the Bar, in some parts of the country, if not here, are degenerating into mere struggles for personal success or pecuniary profit or professional triumph ? and that

the great competition among advocates will soon be—
which of them can most successfully confound and brow-
beat a witness, so as to make him seem to say what he
never did say, or intend to say,—or which of them can
put forth the most cunningly devised fable for cajoling
a jury into a verdict against both the law and the evidence?

It were almost a waste of time to point you to the
Press, in this connection, with a view to enforce or illus-
trate the idea, that nowhere is a more Christian spirit so
sadly needed as in the management of that tremendous
engine for moral good or evil. In that little book, called
"Bonifacius, or Essays to do Good," to the accidental
reading of which our great Bostonian (Benjamin Franklin) ascribed so much of his usefulness in after-life,
Cotton Mather quaintly enjoins upon his readers, that
they should have a strict eye kept upon children, that
"they should not stumble upon the Devil's Library, and
poison themselves with foolish romances or novels, or
plays or songs, or jests that are not convenient." And
if such a caution were needed in New England a century
and a half ago, when neither the Devil nor Dr. Faustus
had found much of a foothold upon our soil,—when the
Printer's Devil, certainly, was confined within a very narrow circuit in our part of the world, and libraries and
books and newspapers of any sort were as rare as they
are now redundant,—how much more need is there of
such a caution in our own times, when the Devil's Library is to be found, dog-cheap, at every corner of our
streets, soliciting the attention of every passer-by by its
proverbial brimstone-colored covers! For one, I hardly

recognize a greater danger to our religious or our civil
institutions, than that which comes from the sapping and
mining process of a flippant, frivolous, licentious, and
infidel literature. It is a danger inseparable from a
country where free opinion, free discussion, and a free
press are enjoyed, and the only defence or safeguard
which can be contemplated for it, is in the inculcation of
a deeper sense of moral and Christian responsibility upon
the minds and hearts of our writers and publishers,
prompting and pressing home upon their consciences
some higher questions, as to their own compositions, or
their own publications, than simply—Will they create a
sensation ?—Will they sell ? It is a hopeless undertaking
to shut out from the sight of our readers, young or old,
whatever is written and published. The very warning
stimulates the curiosity; the very prohibition strengthens
the temptation and points the way to the indulgence. Bible
Societies, and Tract Societies, and Sunday-School Unions
may do something towards diluting them,—I rejoice that
they are doing so much,—but these poisonous and pestilent
streams can only be effectually counteracted at their spring-
head. Marah must be healed at its source. The miracle
of Moses must be repeated, and it is only the righteous
branch which was raised up unto David, which can make
those bitter waters sweet.

I cannot wholly omit in this connection, as a fresh
evidence of what may be feared from intellectual presumption and literary pride and the temptations of
genius,—that the learned author of one of the most
remarkable productions of the English press at the present day, has not hesitated to advance the monstrous doc-

5

trine that Christianity has done nothing for civilization, and that " the religion of mankind is the effect of their improvement, not the cause of it!" How refreshing is it, in contrast with such a doctrine, to turn to what has been said by the greatest living minister of science, the Nestor of Natural History, in closing a chapter of his " Cosmos ":—" In depicting a great epoch in the history of the world,—that of the Empire of the Romans and the laws which they originated, and of the beginning of the Christian religion, (says the illustrious Humboldt,) it was fitting that I should, before all things, recall the manner in which Christianity enlarged the views of mankind, and exercised a mild and enduring, although slowly operating, influence on intelligence and civilization."

But what do you think, my friends, is one of the illustrations which this more recent writer affords us of his own idea of Christianity and religion? Nothing less than an expression of scorn that any intelligent congregation of worshippers should be so blind to the inexorable laws of the physical universe, as to be found offering up " prayers for dry weather or for wet weather!"

A supplication to our Father in heaven that the clouds may once more drop down their dews, to be expunged from our Liturgies, as a vain and foolish superstition!

> " Oh, star-eyed Science, hast thou wandered there,
> To bring us back the tidings of despair!"

A supplication to Almighty God for rain, by a people perishing from drought, a thing to be derided!

So, doubtless, thought that messenger boy, nearly two

thousand years ago, who was sent forward to look toward the sea, while the old Prophet was prostrating himself in prayer, with his face between his knees, upon the top of Carmel. So, doubtless, thought that messenger boy, when again and again, even a fifth and a sixth time, he returned and replied, "There is nothing,—there is nothing,—there is nothing." But that man of God knew in whom he had trusted. He never despaired of the efficacy of prayer even for rain. And, lo, the seventh time, the little cloud was seen rising out of the .sea, like a man's hand, and soon the heavens were black with clouds and wind, and there was a great storm. Even Ahab was compelled to admit that there was something of a shower, and hastened to betake himself to his chariots lest the floods should overwhelm him. And if any one of you, my young friends, finds the memory of that sublime narrative growing faint within him, go and listen to it, whenever you have another opportunity, in its magnificent rendering by Mendelssohn, in the great Oratorio of Elijah, and if you are not unblessed with a total insensibility to the power of music, you will find every chord of your heart trembling and thrilling and vibrating in rapturous response to that almost incomparable chorus, "Thanks be to God, he laveth the thirsty land." I wish that the charming choir behind me could burst into it at this instant. It would be a thousand-fold more effective than any words of mine. For we know where it is written, "With the heart man believes unto righteousness."

Yet better than any mortal music, better than any choral voices of men or of angels,—to silence such a doubt,—comes the calm, clear, simple declaration of Him who spake as never man spake, "Not a sparrow,—not a sparrow falls to the ground without your Father. He sendeth his rain upon the just and upon the unjust. Whatsoever ye shall ask the Father in my name, he will give it you."

I rejoice to reflect, my friends, that this very Fast Day, with its correlative Feast Day at the close of our autumnal season, if they have lost much of their original importance in other respects, still stand on our calendar as witnesses, that we are not quite ready to abandon the faith of our fathers in that great doctrine of the Lord's Prayer,—the special Providence of God. Fast Days, indeed, with so much of the fasting, and humiliation and prayer left out,—Thanksgiving Days, with so little except the turkey and the family frolic left in,—the service of God put forth as a pretext for securing a secular holiday, the livery of Heaven assumed too often to serve the devil in,—these are dismal things to those who look at them deeply and soberly. Yet they still have a significance and a value which should not be underrated, in serving to identify our old Commonwealth, now that so many of the old ear-marks have been carefully erased from our constitution,—as so far forth, at least, a Christian State still, as not to be ashamed to acknowledge by a public act, at seed-time and at harvest time, its dependence upon God for the early and the latter rain, and for all the success which crowns the labors of the husbandman in cultivating those fruits of the earth upon which we rely for our daily bread;—as not ashamed to say, in spite of its habitual and not altogether inexcusable boasting of its own industry and its own invention, "Thou openest thine hand, and fillest all things living with plenteousness!"

I should feel myself justly chargeable with a grave omission, in a discourse dealing so plainly with the want of a more Christian spirit, and motive, and principle, in so many lines of life, were I to make no reference to the manner in which our political concerns are conducted ;— were I to bear no testimony, where, perhaps, in years not long past, I might have been summoned as an expert, and where I may still expose myself to the suggestion of having only turned State's evidence.

We often hear predictions of the overthrow of our civil institutions as the inevitable result of this or that measure of executive policy, or of this or that course of legislative or of party action. And I am not insensible myself to the danger that our domestic peace may at some time or other be interrupted, and even our Union practically sundered, by the violence and virulence with which sectional interests are so often arrayed against each other, and the peculiar institutions of different portions of the country attacked or defended. But a far, far more serious subject for alarm to every Christian patriot must be found, I think, in the political corruption which has of late been growing and spreading like a leprosy over our land. No one can have observed the proceedings of parties or of politicians, whether in power or out of power, during the last few years, without perceiving that anything like Christian principle in politics is getting to be less and less a matter of consideration or even of recognition,—that any pretence to it, indeed, is beginning to be more and more a theme for scorn and derision,—that every measure, and almost every man, is considered as having a price,—and that everything is regarded as fair to be attempted, and as fit to be done, which may conduce to ultimate success. To secure a triumph for one's party, to get office for one's self or one's friend, have become the almost undisguised objects of ambition and effort, and no means have been held disreputable,—no bargain, barter, false pretence, or false accusation,—which could be serviceable to this end.

"In old times (said the excellent Judge Gaston of North Carolina, in the Convention for amending the Constitution of his own State),—in old times, an application for office was an extraordinary occurrence. During the four years which he spent in Congress, but one application was made to him on the subject, and that (says he) came from, perhaps, the most despicable of his constituents. The letter was somewhat in this fashion: 'I and my friends have constantly supported you. The times are hard and I want a post; and I don't much care what post it is, so that it has a good salary attached to it.' It is needless to state my answer, (continues that great and good judge;) but I was strongly tempted to inform him that there was but one post for which I could recommend him,—and that was the Whipping Post."

Alas, how deplorably have the times changed,—I should rather say, have men changed,—in this respect! It seems to be forgotten that the robes of office must be fairly and purely won, as well as worthily and gracefully worn, or they are no robes of honor; and that not even the strength of a Hercules could survive the contact of that worse than poisoned shirt of Nessus—an official robe procured by foul play or false professions, or even by mere mendicancy. They seem to have forgotten the justice and beauty of that grand idea of an old poet :—

> " High worth is elevated place ; 'tis more,
> It makes the post stand candidate for thee."

We have seen an occasional, and, I doubt not, a well-intended effort, here and there, to arrest the progress of this political plague by the direct interposition of the clergy, and the open participation of the pulpit in the discussions of the election room. But thus far, instead of carrying religion into politics, they seem only to have succeeded in carrying politics into religion. The mingling of ministers of the Gospel in the conflicts of party can do little, I fear, to raise the character of the hustings, —while it is certain it may do much to lower the dignity and impair the influence of the pulpit.

The clergy must, indeed, follow out their own conscientious convictions of duty without fear or favor, so far as man is concerned. Neither popular displeasure nor popular applause must control their topics, nor modify their treatment of them. They must not prophesy unto us smooth things, nor shrink from declaring the whole counsel of God, as it is revealed to their own waiting hearts. Through them the Gospel must have free course and be glorified ; and it is for us to submit ourselves meekly to their rebukes, if by any chance we shall at any time give occasion to them. Yet as one who honors their vocation and would ever see it honored ;—as one who believes that the best interests of mankind are bound

up with the maintenance of an independent and faithful
ministry ;—as one who is convinced that from the Church
of Christ are to be primarily derived the richest blessings
to be enjoyed in this world or to be hoped in another, and
that there is no security for morality, and no safeguard
for liberty, but in religious faith and fear, promoted and
inculcated through the earnest preaching of the Word of
God ;—I cannot help deploring for the past, and depre-
cating for the future, that sort of secular disputation and
political discussion in the pulpit, which tends only to the
distraction and division of whole congregations of good
men, and which has furnished the example under which
this very platform, and others like it, are beginning to be
used on the Lord's day for the repetition of Lyceum lectures by laymen.

I know there are honest differences of opinion on these
subjects. I do not forget that some of us are open to
the imputation of objecting to pulpit discussions of this
sort, not because ministers preach politics, but because
they do not preach what we may happen to consider the
right side. And perhaps I may even now subject myself
to the easy retort, that pulpit politics are no more out of
place than lay preaching. But it is more than enough
even to have referred to such shallow suggestions. I
make no question of the sincerity and of the sense of duty
under which everything is said that is said, and everything done, that is done ; and I ask only the same respect
for my own judgment which I freely and fully accord to
others ;—but I should be false to one of the deepest convictions of my heart, were I to refrain, on this occasion,
from an honest and earnest expression of the idea,—that

even Domestic Slavery, as it is known in some parts of
our own land, will never have inflicted a more fatal
wound upon the hopes of humanity, even upon those
hopes of humanity which are in any quarter associated
with its own ultimate disappearance, than when it shall
have succeeded in rending the seamless garment, and in
riving asunder the Church of Christ. Nor, in my humble judgment, will those who deride and denounce that
Church ever find so effective a wedge for severing it in
twain, and shivering it into fragments, as in the intro-
duction of the slavery discussion into our various religious associations.

I cannot forget, in this connection, my young friends,
that when I myself first entered upon political life, more
than a quarter of a century ago, it was common, even in
Puritan New England, to hold grand party gatherings
on the evening of the Sabbath. It was, indeed, the favorite night for such occasions just before an election, and
there was always an eager competition for the use of
Faneuil Hall for the purpose. I have heard Otis and
Quincy and Webster speak there on a Sunday night, and
—as this is a day for humiliation and confession,—I must
not omit to say that I believe I once spoke there myself
on that evening. It has been justly regarded as a great
moral and social and religious reform to have abolished
the custom, and our election days have been thrown over
from Monday to Tuesday, partly, if not wholly, to pre-
vent the temptation of using any portion of the Lord's
day in electioneering preparations. But in vain shall we
have discarded Sunday night caucuses, if the morning or
afternoon services of the sanctuary are to be perverted to

the use of politics, and if the prayers of the House of God
are only to be grudgingly served out, like a hurried grace
before meat, as a prelude to an electioneering appeal or a
political diatribe. " The Lord is in his holy temple, let
all the earth keep silence before Him ; "—this is the language of the sacred volume, as well as the appropriate
and impressive opening of the Episcopal Liturgy ;—and
I know of no better or juster interpretation of the passage than that which I rejoice to say it seems generally
to have received in my own Church,—that all earthly
controversies and contentions should be hushed—hushed
—in the house consecrated to the worship of God.

No, my friends, the disease to which I have been allud-
ing is one, and the remedy must be one :—Diversities of
operations, but the same Spirit. If a higher and purer
principle in politics, if a loftier integrity on the Exchange
or at the Bar, if a worthier management of the Press, if
a less intemperate and reckless policy in pressing forward
the cause of moral and social reform, if all or any of these
consummations are to be witnessed in our day, as God
grant they may be,—or in any day,—it will not be
because the Pulpit shall have abandoned the great topics
of the Gospel and the great doctrines of salvation for any
secular discussions whatever. It will rather be, because
holding fast to its legitimate work of preaching Christ
and Him crucified, and unfolding with renewed energy
from week to week those two great Commandments upon
which hang all the law and all the prophets—love to God
and love to man,—the pulpit shall have succeeded in
awakening the great masses of the community, and especially in arousing the minds of the young, to higher

and nobler views of Christian duty. It will be because individual men and women,—prompted and animated by such appeals from the pulpit, and aided and enlightened by that Holy Spirit which is ever ready to help our infirmities, and to quicken us in every good way and work, if we will but open our hearts to its influences,—shall associate themselves together, as you have done, for the adoption and cultivation of a more Christian spirit and a more Christian principle in all the various walks of life. It will not be because the pursuits and controversies of the week-day have been carried into the discourses of the Sabbath, but because more of the spirit of the Sabbath, and of Him who was Lord of the Sabbath, has been brought into the business of the week-day ;—because, in a word, more of the Divine Life has been incorporated into the daily life of those by whom the affairs and relations of mankind are regulated and conducted.

For it is not enough, my young friends, for you to have adopted a good name for your association. It is not enough for any of us merely to profess and call ourselves Christians. Almost the whole civilized world, indeed, has long assumed to itself the title of the Christian world ; and it rejoices in the recognition of the Christian era as the period from which all human acts or ordinances are dated. We set down, each one of us, on every written or printed page, at the top of every letter of business or note of friendship, of every bill or *billet doux*, the year of our Lord,—as if there were no time worthy to be counted in our calendar (as, in very truth, there is not) until Christ appeared upon the earth to bring life and immortality to light ;—as if time were nothing, as in truth it is nothing, except when regarded as the vestibule of an assured eternity,—the first infant step of a never-ending and immortal career. But how much of this is formal, fashionable, a matter of routine, or a matter of reckoning! How few of us, as we date our notes or our letters 1858 or 1859, consider or care, or even remember, from what event so many hundred years have passed away without detracting one jot or one tittle from its infinite and unutterable importance! Christmas comes and goes, and comes again, with the revolution of the seasons. The usual amount of feasting and dancing, of family gatherings and friendly present-makings, is sure to be witnessed. The churches are decorated, the windows are festooned, the evergreen-tree is lighted with candles and loaded with *souvenirs*, and a " merry Christmas " is the unfailing ejaculation of every man to his neighbor. But amidst all this anniversary gayety and conventional gladness, how many of us think seriously of the momentous character of the occasion we celebrate! How many pause from their merry sports to ask themselves the solemn question,—Has Christ really ever been born to us? Have we ever been with the wise men to worship at his cradle, or with the loving women to bend before his cross? We have used his birthday as an occasion for bringing gifts to others; have we ever employed it in bringing gifts to Him,—even the homage of a grateful heart? As an historical fact, we all of us know that He came into the world more than eighteen centuries and a half ago; that he was wrapped in swaddling clothes and cradled in a manger; that he taught, and suffered, and died. But is it not one thing to recognize the birth of Christ historically, and to use it as a convenient starting-point in the calculation of time,—and a widely different thing to recognize it individually, personally, and as one's own immediate concern,—feeling, as each successive day of the Nativity comes round, that we are commemorating the birth of one whose right it is to reign supreme in every heart, and to whose dominion our own heart acknowledges a willing, joyful, and undivided allegiance? When that great advent and incarnation shall be recognized and celebrated in this spirit,—when it shall even be recognized in our religious calendar with as much of earnest loyalty as the birthday of Washington is beginning to be recognized in our political calendar,—the day will not be so distant, as now it is, when the kingdoms of this world shall become, in fact as well as of right, the kingdoms of our Lord and of his Christ. But as the world goes now, it may well be feared that to not a few of those who boast themselves of the title of Christians, it may be said, hereafter, by the great Author and Finisher of our faith, in the striking language of one of the ancient prophets,—" I have *surnamed* thee, though thou hast not known me."

Doubtless even this formal recognition of Christianity is not altogether without its practical value. It is something,—it is much,—for young men, especially, to have voluntarily adopted that name for their watchword, and to find them thus countenancing and encouraging each other in overcoming the shamefacedness with which a religious profession is too often entered upon, in Protestant communities. But the Christian spirit, breathing through the individual soul, the Christian motive in-

forming and actuating the personal life, the Christian
principle guiding, governing, controlling the thought,
word, act of every day and hour,—these are what con-
stitute the real recognition and adoption of the name of
Christ, and these are what every man, young or old,
pledges himself to aim at and strive for, who voluntarily
enlists in the ranks of a Christian church, or a Christian association. The Christian life, as nobly set forth
by Thomas Arnold of Rugby,—as beautifully delineated
by Peter Bayne of Edinburgh,—as humbly but heroically
exemplified by Howard, and Heber, and Chalmers, and
Wilberforce, and Samuel Budgett, and John Foster, and
Lady Huntingdon, and Elizabeth Gurney, better known
as Mrs. Fry,—as admirably commended before the Queen
of England by John Caird of Errol,—as exquisitely anal-
yzed by Wesley in the successive stanzas of that almost
matchless hymn—" Jesus, my strength, my hope,"—
as perfectly personified by Jesus himself, and by him
alone, in his walk upon earth;—this Christian life, this
life of Christ,—and no mere empty historical acknowl-
edgment of a date, or a name, or an event,—is what you,
Young Men, have associated yourselves to promote and
cultivate in yourselves and others ;—and this it is, which,
promoted and cultivated earnestly and successfully, will,
in the good time of Him, with whom a thousand years
is as one day, reform the abuses of the world, so far as
they are ever destined to be reformed here, and prepare
the way for the coming of those new heavens and that
new earth, wherein dwelleth righteousness.

And how, let me inquire for a moment, how, my
friends, does this Christian life differ from the common
life of those around you ?

There is no more mistaken view, certainly, of the Christian life, than that which represents it as a life of separation and seclusion from the business of the world, and from the performance, by each one of us, of that part in the transactions of society, which may have been assigned to us by Providence. The day is past,—never to return, I trust, in this region of the globe,—when anything of monastic retirement and solitude is to be counted among the dictates of Christian duty. On the contrary, the requirements of a true Christian obligation demand that every man should be in the world, among his fellowmen, doing good to all within his reach, and serving his country and his community in every way in his power. Even the ancient heathen philosophy did not admit the idea of such a thing as the possibility of an escape from duty. "For no part of life," says Cicero most nobly, —"whether you are employed in private or in public affairs,—whether you are doing anything by yourself or negotiating anything with others,—can be free from duty ; and in observing that is all the honor, and in neglecting that is all the disgrace of life." And not less nobly says the Christian poet of the Lakes :—

> " Powers depart,
> Possessions vanish, and opinions change,
> And passions hold a fluctuating seat ;—
> But by the storm of circumstance unshaken,
> And subject neither to eclipse nor wane,
> Duty exists."

The duties of life are to be discharged, not shrunk from nor shirked. The world is to be carried along, and the business of the world, with all its petty cares, and with all its momentous concerns. Lands are to be tilled, houses built, trade conducted, government administered, justice executed,—education, literature, science, and every useful art, promoted and advanced. The Christian life, in a word, is to be engrafted upon the daily life, not cherished and cultivated as a thing apart and independent.

It is not easy to overestimate the value of Sunday to the Christian world, and I would be the last to have anything of its sacredness diminished, or any of its holy time encroached upon. Yet it cannot be denied that the very strictness of its observance has had a tendency to encourage an idea, that religion is a peculiar thing, to be reserved exclusively for a separate season and a particular day,—that prayers are only for churches or funerals, and piety to be put on and thrown off with our Sunday suits. But the true Christian will so far at least recognize every day as the Lord's day, as to carry his Christian principles and his Christian spirit into every sphere of occupation, and even of recreation and amusement. For we all know that amusements and recreations there must be,—a time to laugh as well as a time to weep or to be serious ;— and I doubt extremely the wisdom of limiting the variety of amusements, for young or old, by too Puritanic a standard. A religious heart will reject all such amusements as are inconsistent with its own peace and its own purity ; but a formal, rigid, arbitrary proscription of particular amusements will not create a religious heart. It is more likely to create an irreligious, impatient, rebellious one.

But even into the sphere of social recreations and amusements a Christian spirit, a spirit of moderation and

temperance, of mutual deference and politeness, of true
gentility and nobility,—for all these belong to the best
elements of the Christian character,—may be, and ought
to be, and will be carried. Under their influence the relations and associations of the sexes will assume a more
dignified and refined, though by no means a less cheerful
footing ; the pervading and prevailing spirit of selfishness
and sensuality will be exorcised ; and those flaunting and
frivolous gallantries will disappear, which threaten to turn
even the sacred tie of matrimony into nothing better than
a mere *beau-knot*. The shameless doctrine of affinities
superior to marriage-vows, will be strangled in its cradle,
and we shall be spared the horror of scenes like those
which have recently made us almost ready to disown and
forswear the capital of our country. Young America,
too, will be less eager to signalize itself in inventing and
employing derisive appellations for parents and elders,
and the good old words, "father and mother," will
resume their sacred significance in the daily domestic
vocabulary. A tyrannical fashion, too, will abate somewhat of its preposterous exactions and its absurd pre-
scriptions, and will at least take care to accommodate the
hoops of its votaries to the dimensions of our pew-doors.

There is a most remarkable passage, my friends, in
Paley's celebrated " Essay on the Evidences of Christianity," which is worthy of being listened to even as a
specimen of the most felicitous and forcible style, and
which contains sentiments certainly entitled to the grav-
est consideration :—

" The influence of religion," says he, " is not to be
sought for in the councils of princes, in the debates or

7

resolutions of popular assemblies, in the conduct of governments towards their subjects, or of states and sovereigns towards one another ; of conquerors at the head of their armies, or of parties intriguing for power at home, (topics which alone almost occupy the attention, and fill the pages of history ;)—but must be perceived, if perceived at all, in the silent course of private and domestic life. Nay more ; even *there* its influence may not be very obvious to observation. If it check, in some degree, personal dissoluteness, if it beget a general probity in the transaction of business, if it produce soft and humane manners in the mass of the community, and occasional exertions of laborious or expensive benevolence in a few individuals, it is all the effect which can offer itself to external notice. *The kingdom of heaven is within us.* That which is the substance of the religion, its hopes and consolations, its intermixture with the thoughts by day and by night, the devotion of the heart, the control of the appetite, the steady direction of the will to the commands of God, is necessarily invisible. Yet upon these depend the virtue and the happiness of millions. This cause renders the representations of history, with respect to religion, defective and fallacious, in a greater degree than they are upon any other subject.—Religion operates most upon those of whom history knows the least ; upon fathers and mothers in their families, upon men servants and maid servants, upon the orderly tradesman, the quiet villager, the manufacturer at his loom, the husbandman in his fields. Amongst such, its influence collectively may be of inestimable value, yet its effects, in the mean time, little upon those who figure upon the stage of the world. *They* may know nothing of it ; they may believe nothing of it ; they may be actuated by motives more impetuous than those which religion is able to excite. It cannot therefore be thought strange that this influence should elude the grasp and touch of public history ; for what is public history, but a register of the successes and disappointments, the vices, the follies, and the quarrels of those who engage in contentions for power ? "

True, indeed,—alas, too true,—is this eloquent and masterly analysis of the influence of religion, as manifested in the history of the world, when Paley penned it and published it, more than sixty years ago ; and I fear that the more than half a century which has since elapsed, boastful as it has been of its progress in civilization and Christianity, has done little to diminish its accuracy. It is still in the daily decencies and proprieties and integrities and purities of private and social life that the influences of religious faith and fear are to be most distinctly, if not altogether and exclusively, looked for ; and if they should ever fail to be found and recognized there, we may, indeed, begin to despair of their efficacy anywhere, over the human heart. But Heaven forbid, that we should accept this as the predestined and unalterable current of history in all time to come ! Why, why shall not the influence of religion be sought for, and be found, in the councils of princes, in the debates and resolutions of popular assemblies, in the conduct of governments towards their subjects and towards one another ? Why shall it not be sought for, and be found, in the conduct of conquerors at the head of their armies abroad, and of parties, not " intriguing," indeed, but honorably striving for

power at home? Why shall any who figure on the stage
of the world know nothing of religion, believe nothing of
it, and be actuated by motives more impetuous than any
which religion is able to excite? And why, why shall
public history continue to be only a register of the vices
and follies and quarrels of those who engage in contentions for power?

But let us hear Paley once more, in another of his
most impressive and powerful passages, before I conclude
this discourse by a brief reply to these questions:—

" The truth is," says he, " (and pity 'tis, 'tis true,) there
are two opposite descriptions of character, under which
mankind may generally be classed. The one possesses
vigor, firmness, resolution ; is daring and active, quick in
its sensibilities, jealous of its fame, eager in its attach-
ments, inflexible in its purposes, violent in its resentments ;
the other, meek, yielding, complying, forgiving,—not
prompt to act, but willing to suffer,—silent and gentle
under rudeness and insult, suing for reconciliation where
others would demand satisfaction, giving way to the
pushes of impudence, conceding and indulgent to the
prejudices, the wrongheadedness, the intractability of
those with whom it has to deal.

"The former of these characters is, and ever hath been,
the favorite of the world. It is the character of great
men. There is a dignity in it which universally commands respect. The latter is poor-spirited, tame, and
abject. Yet so it hath happened, that, with the Founder
of Christianity, this latter is the subject of his commen-
dation, his precepts, his example; and that the former is
so in no part of its composition. This, (he maintains,)

and nothing else, is the character designed in the follow
ing remarkable passages : ' Resist not evil ; but whosoever shall smite thee on the right cheek, turn to him the
other also ; and if any man will sue thee at the law, and
take away thy coat, let him have thy cloak also ; and
whosoever shall compel thee to go a mile, go with him
twain; love your enemies, bless them that curse you, do
good to them that hate you, and pray for them which
despitefully use you and persecute you.' This certainly
(says he) is not commonplace morality. It shows at
least, (and it is for this purpose we produce it,) that no
two things can be more different than the Heroic and
the Christian character."

No two things more different than the Heroic and the
Christian character ! I will not pause to ask where was
Paley's remembrance of those earlier and later martyrs
of Christianity, who submitted themselves without flinch-
ing to the fury of the lions or the raging of the flames.
Was there no heroism there ? I will not pause to ask
where was his remembrance of Stephen or of Paul, of
Ridley or of Latimer,—of Cranmer, thrusting his right
hand into the fire that it might be burned to cinders first
and alone, because it had offended by writing a recanta-
tion of the truth,—or of poor Lady Jane Grey, whose
unshaken constancy to the cause of Christ has stirred the
sympathy of so many hearts, and drawn tears from so
many eyes, during the more than three centuries which
have elapsed since her youthful form was laid upon the
block. Was there no heroism there? I will not pause
to suggest that the profound and eloquent moralist has
pressed his contrast to an extreme, in speaking of the

Christian character as ever necessarily "poor-spirited, tame, and abject," in the reproachful sense in which those epithets would now be understood. Let me rather ask again, is this discouraging and fearful contrast one of perpetual necessity? Is it written irrevocably in the book of destiny, that quick and jealous and quarrelsome men, inflexible in purpose, and violent in resentment, are forever to be the favorites of the world, are always to be the great men of the world? Is it written unchangeably in the book of destiny, that those who figure on the pages of history are to know nothing of religion, to believe nothing of religion, and to be actuated by motives more impetuous than any which religion can excite? I fear that not a few of those who aspire to be the great men of the world, even in this day and generation, may have shaped their course upon such an hypothesis. But have there not been those already, who seem to have risen up —to have been raised up, let me rather say—to change the standard of human greatness, and who have changed it, since these passages were composed by Paley, more than sixty years ago? Are there no figures even in our own American history, which lift themselves majestically before us as we speak, to attest the possibility that there may be such a thing as ingrafting the Christian character upon the Heroic character, and blending them into an harmonious and matchless unity? Shall we admit that the character of Washington was anything less than heroic, anything other than Christian? Was there no union of the Heroic and the Christian character in the youthful Kane, braving those repeated winters of disease and darkness in those "thrilling regions of thick-ribb'd ice,"

ever offering up his little prayer—"Lord, accept our
gratitude and bless our undertaking," or " Return us to
our homes,"—and still reminding his despairing comrades
how often an Unseen Power had rescued them in peril,
and admonishing them still to place reliance on Him who
could not change!

Cross the ocean, too, and gather with your Saxon
brethren around the tomb of the brave Sir Henry Law-
rence, or the lamented Havelock, or the youthful Vicars,
or unite in the homage which is everywhere paid to those
lovely, living Sisters of Charity, with Florence Nightin-
gale at their head, braving those burning climes, and
breathing that tainted air, while they ministered to the
bodies and the souls of those dying soldiers,—and tell
me whether these are not examples which will illumi-
nate the brightest pages of modern history, or of any
history; and bear perpetual testimony that the highest
heroism is no longer incompatible with the truest Christianity!

O, yes, my young friends, it is not too late,—you
can still redeem history from the reproach of being only
the register of the vices, follies, and quarrels of those
who are contending for power. The influence of religion
may still, by God's blessing, be sought for and be found,
in the councils of princes and even of presidents, in the
debates and resolutions of popular assemblies, and even
of Parliaments, and of Congresses,—in the conduct of
conquerors at the head of their armies, and even of parties in the heat of their strife. The day may still come,
when the highest illustration of the heroic character will
be recognized in the conquest not of others but of one's

self;—when the greatest heroes will be acknowledged to
be those who have won single-handed victories in the
unseen battle-fields of their own souls, with no witnesses
but God and the angels; and when we shall all realize
the truth of that saying which poor Sheridan (seeing and
describing the glory which, alas, he could not achieve for
himself,) has put into the mouth of his Rolla : " To
triumph o'er ourselves is the only conquest where fortune
makes no claim. In battle chance may snatch the laurel
from thee, or chance may place it on thy brow ; but in a
contest with thyself be resolute, and the virtuous impulse
must be the victor." The day may still come, when the
Heroic and the Christian character, blended into one, shall
be hailed as the only consummation, which is possible in
this sublunary state, of the cherished idea of a perfected
humanity, and when the world shall do willing homage
to the men and the women who shall display these
hitherto contrasted and conflicting elements in the most
complete and harmonious combination.

And you, my friends, have invented or adopted the
precise enginery by which this fusion is to be effected,
and this glorious change accomplished. Let the great
mass of the young men of America organize themselves
into associations like that before me, and persevere sys-
tematically and conscientiously in pursuing the ends
which this Association has proposed to itself, and the
time will come when, to their united efforts, will be traced
a reformation of manners and morals, of opinion and of
practice, of social, of professional, and of political life,
compared with which all other reformations or revo-
lutions will have been only so many precursors and

pioneers,—only so many voices crying in the wilderness, " Prepare ye the way of the Lord ! "

Our illustrious Franklin, while still a printer at Philadelphia, on the 9th of May, 1731, being then about five-and-twenty years old, recorded the result of his " observations on reading history " in the library which he had founded, in the following words : " There seems to me at present to be great occasion for raising *a United Party for Virtue*, by forming the virtuous and good men of all nations into a regular body, to be governed by suitable, good, and wise rules, which good and wise men may, probably, be more unanimous in their obedience to, than common people are to common laws." It may have been a fanciful speculation on Franklin's part, and the virtue which he contemplated may hardly have had enough of the Christian element in it, to give it consistency or stability. But the idea, in its best interpretation, seems almost realized and accomplished by the affiliated Young Men's Christian Associations which have recently been spread over so many parts of our country and of the world. A United Party for Christian Virtue has thus been organized. More than twenty thousand young men are estimated to have joined it already in the United States alone. It has no personal or political aims. It rallies to no elections. It seeks no spoils or offices. It appeals to no individual or even national prejudices. It looks to no sectional or sectarian triumphs. It raises no flag, blazoned with the emblems of mere worldly, earthly, temporal interests. But taking the Bible, the open Bible, as its platform, and lifting the Cross as its ensign, " putting on the breastplate of faith and love, and

for a helmet, the hope of salvation," it goes forth to
wrestle with " the rulers of the darkness of this world,
against spiritual wickedness in high places." And who
doubts that God will go forth with such an army, and
that " his banner over it will be Love ? " Who doubts
that, if faithful to itself, and yielding to no temptations to
embark in secular enterprises or controversies, it will go
on " conquering and to conquer," and that from line to
line, from wing to wing, of its marshalled and embattled
legions, shall be heard the triumphant song, " Thou hast
given a banner to them that fear Thee, that it may be dis-
played because of the truth. Through God we shall
do valiantly, for He it is that shall tread down our
enemies ! "

And shall there be longer a doubt, that a body of
young men, numbering hardly less than two thousand in
our own city, thus associated, in such a spirit, and for
these high and holy ends, shall have the means of securing for themselves every accommodation which they may
need, or may reasonably ask ? Shall there be a longer
delay in providing them with convenient apartments and
an ample hall in which they may carry on their great
work of moral and spiritual improvement,—writing on
its walls—Salvation—and on its gates—Praise !

The atmosphere around us, I know, is at this moment
filled almost to suffocation with projects, some of them
gigantic projects, mammoth projects, for erecting edifices
for every variety of purpose. The brain reels, and the
most sanguine and liberal heart almost despairs, at the
proposals and applications which are multiplied at every
turn. Yonder "Back Bay" will have more than fulfilled

the largest promise of its name, if it shall prove strong
enough to bear even one half the load which seems destined
to be imposed upon it. Art and science, education and
literature, natural history and civil history, patriotism
and charity, severally and jointly, have been beseeching
and besieging our public and our private treasuries for
aid. Gladly, most gladly, would I see them all successful,—not all at once, perhaps, but each in its order. Let
Charity be aided in building up her hospitals and her
homes for the orphan and the widow, for the indigent
and the sick, curable and incurable. Let Patriotism be
encouraged in preserving the memorials and monuments
and precious relics of the great and good men, who
planted our colony, or achieved our independence, or
who have illustrated our constitutional history. Let the
Home and the Grave of Washington never be the property of anything less than the whole Union. Let central
and convenient Armories not be withheld from the old
battalions or the new battalions, whose interposition with
the arm of flesh may be needed, we know not how soon,
to execute our laws or maintain our domestic peace.
Let Education and Learning and Literature enjoy a
liberal patronage for their schools, and colleges, and
academies, and libraries. Let Art, in due time, have
her galleries and repositories and conservatories, for all
that mechanic invention and philosophical ingenuity and
the most cultured and refined taste and skill, in marble
or in bronze or on the canvas, can design or accomplish.
Let the Natural Sciences have their spacious corridors
and cabinets for the preservation and display of everything
that is rare, and recondite, and curious in the air above,

or in the earth beneath, or in the waters under the earth,
—where old and young may observe and study the works
of God in Nature, and where their hearts may be exalted
towards the great Creator. I rejoice that this object at
least, is secured—that this is to be done first of all and
without delay, so that not a day of the remaining life, of
that eminent adopted Naturalist of ours,—Agassiz,—
whom the fascinations and blandishments of foreign
courts have not been able to seduce from his chosen allegiance to the cause of American science,—so that not a
day of his life, even should it be, as we hope, as long as
that of his illustrious friend Humboldt, may be lost to
mankind through our neglect ; and so that not one of all
the myriad specimens which he has so laboriously col-
lected may perish for want of a safe place of deposit.
Religion has nothing to fear from science. Nature and
revelation—what are they but two volumes of the same
Divine Book ? "Between the Word and the Works of
God, (said the lamented Hugh Miller,) there can be no
actual discrepancies; and the seeming ones are discern-
ible only by the men who see worst.

> 'Mote-like they flicker in unsteady eyes,
> And weakest his who best descries ? ' "

But neither science nor art, nor education nor literature, nor natural history nor civil history, nor patriotism,
nor even charity itself, can supply any substitute for religion. There is a higher revelation, and one more worthy
of our best study, than even the record of the Rocks or the
testimony of the Turtles. Nay, there have been rents in
the rocks themselves, which have attested more momentous things than any which geology can ever teach,—

even should its excavations, with more than Artesian
enterprise, strike down upon the very central fires, and
uncover them before their time! There is a first and
great commandment superior even to the second which
is like unto it. There is a better country even than
our native land. There is a more glorious liberty
even than American Liberty. There is a more consecrated mount even than Mount Vernon. And these
young men whose faces are set towards the Mount
Zion, who, without renouncing one particle of love or
loyalty to the land in which they live, yet seek to secure
a future citizenship in another country—even a heavenly
—and who would fain improve themselves and others in
things which pertain to their everlasting portion and
peace,—let it never be said that their moderate and
reasonable claims were postponed to any which have
been, or to any which can be, named. Let it never
be said, that while schemes are on foot which might
almost carry us along to the grandeur and magnificence
of another Antioch, those who are calling themselves
Christians are left without a home. If we grudged
not the cost of rescuing the remains of a gallant company of foreign navigators from their icy shrouds on the
Arctic shores,—how can we withhold the means of rescuing the souls of our living sons from the frozen realms
of infidelity or indifference, or from the torrid zone of
sensuality and crime! Let Religion ever have that rightful preëminence among us which is symbolized in the
stately towers and soaring spires of her churches. Let
science and art and education and patriotism be ever
encircled and glorified with a halo of holiness from the